Will You Read to Me?

Atheneum Books for Young Readers
An imprint of Simon & Schuster Children's Publishing Division
1230 Avenue of the Americas
New York, New York 10020
Copyright © 2007 by Denys Cazet
All rights reserved, including the right of reproduction in whole
or in part in any form.
Book design by Sonia Chaghatzbanian
The text for this book is set in Egyptian 710.
The illustrations for this book are rendered in watercolor and
colored pencil.
Manufactured in China

10 9 8 7 6 5 4 3
Library of Congress Cataloging-in-Publication Data
Cazet, Denys.
Will you read to me? / Denys Cazet.—1st ed.
p. cm.
"A Richard Jackson Book."
Summary: Hamlet enjoys reading books and writing poetry, not
playing in the mud and fighting over supper like the other pigs,
but he finally finds someone who appreciates him just as he is.
ISBN-13: 978-1-4169-0935-4
ISBN-10: 1-4169-0935-4
[1. Individuality—Fiction. 2. Pigs—Fiction. 3. Books and
reading—Fiction.] I. Title.
PZ7.C2985Wil 2007
[E]—dc22
2005024144

Story and pictures by **Denys Cazet**

Will You Read to Me?

A Richard Jackson Book

Atheneum Books for Young Readers

New York London Toronto Sydney

For Donna

Hamlet leaned over the fence.
He looked at all the pigs, soaking in the mud.
"Mom?" he said. "Dad?"

A big pig looked up. "Yes, dear?" said his mother.

"I have a new book," said Hamlet. "Will you read to me?"

Hamlet's father sat up. "Is it a cookbook?" he asked.

"No," said Hamlet. "It's about a dragon that doesn't want to be one."

"Oh," said his father.
He rolled over
into a warm spot.

Hamlet showed his mother his notebook.
"I wrote some poems," he said.
"I can read to you."

"Poems," said his sister. "What kind of pig writes poems?"
"What kind of pig wears a clean shirt?" said a brother.
"Look, Ma. There's not a spot on it."

Hamlet tried to cover
the shirt with his notebook.
"It's a good thing
there aren't two of him!"
someone said.
"Twins," said his big brother.
"Hamlet and Eggs."

Just as everyone started to laugh,
they saw the farmer walking away
from the eating trough.

"Supper!"

they shouted
and shoved
and pushed
their way across
the mud hole.

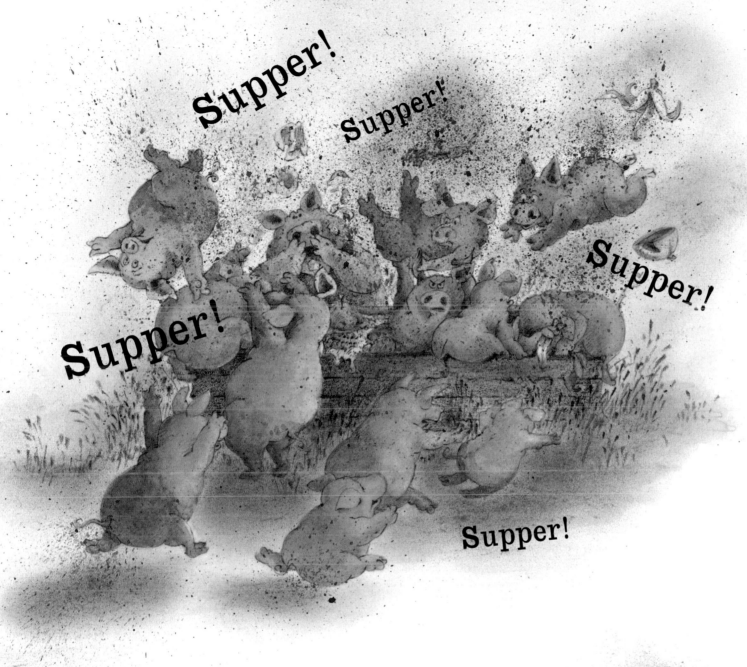

Supper! Supper! Supper! Supper! Supper!

Supper!

Hamlet looked at the pigsty.
He didn't feel very hungry.
He looked at a spot of mud
on his favorite shirt,
and then walked away.

When he saw the farmer's pond
he stopped for a moment
and watched the rising moon.

He sat down near
the edge of the water
and wrote a new poem
in his notebook.

When he looked into the pond
he saw his twin looking back.

"Oh!" he gasped.
"It's you."
Hamlet waved.
His twin waved.
"Do you mind if I
call you Eggs?"
Hamlet asked.

Eggs didn't answer.
"I'll read to you," said Hamlet,
"and then you can read to me."

Can there be such a thing as
Pigness without the dirt?
Or am I, Hamlet, just . . . a sort-of pig
with mud on his favorite shirt?

Hamlet looked into the water again.
The wind ruffled the surface
of the pond.

Hamlet's twin bobbed up
and down in the moonlight.
"Oh, good," he said. "I'm glad you liked it.
Now it's your turn."

Black leaves drifted in the fading sky,
and shadows crept along the edge of the pond.
The frogs began their nightly chorus, and an owl hooted.
The breeze rattled the cattails, brushed Hamlet's face,
and then it was quiet.

"Very nice," said Hamlet.
"I wrote a poem about the wind.
I'll read it to you."

The wind is rising with the moon,
like whispers from a tender ghost—
an October wind,
soft and warm,
gently moving through the garden.

Listen.
Can you hear the sound
of brushed silk, sitting by the window?
Shhh.
Listen.

"Did you get it?" Hamlet asked.
"Brushed silk is the fur of a black cat
I saw sitting by the farmer's window."

The little pig looked into the water
just as a cloud drifted across the moon.

Hamlet's twin began to fade away.
"Oh!" said Hamlet.

"Don't go.
See if you like this one better.
It's about cantaloupe."

The moon is a cold,
sweet slice of cantaloupe
sitting on a porcelain plate,
ready to be carved
by the constellation **Spoon**.

Hamlet looked into the pond. It was dark.
"Oh," he said sadly. "Good-bye, Eggs.
I guess you didn't like that one either."

Hamlet sat down.

"I liked it," said a small voice.

"Me too," said another. "We all did."

Hamlet looked up. "Oh my," he said.

"Will you read to us?" they asked.